Liam Wins the Game, Sometimes

Sometimes

A Story about Losing with Grace

Jane Whelen Banks

Jessica Kingsley Publishers
London and Philadelphia

First published in 2009
by Jessica Kingsley Publishers
116 Pentonville Road
London N1 9JB, UK
and
400 Market Street, Suite 400
Philadelphia, PA 19106, USA

www.jkp.com

Library of Congress Cataloging in Publication Data
Banks, Jane Whelen.
  Liam wins the game, sometimes : a story about losing with grace / Jane Whelen Banks.
      p. cm.
  ISBN 978-1-84310-898-6 (pb : alk. paper) 1. Sportsmanship--Juvenile literature. I. Title.
  GV706.3.B36 2009
  175--dc22

                              2008017769

British Library Cataloguing in Publication Data
A CIP catalogue record for this book is available from the British Library

ISBN 978 1 84310 898 6

Printed and bound in China by
Reliance Printing Co, Ltd.

Dedication

To my husband Peter, whose youthful enthusiasm
for play has not been forgotten.

Learning to play games is fundamental to growing up. Through games, a child can learn to organize himself, follow rules, plan strategies, and negotiate while gaining valuable knowledge and skills. Games can also offer a structured social forum that may soothe even the most awkward soul. With a clear set of instructions, their predictability brings comfort to those individuals less adept at navigating free time with others. In addition to observing the guidelines of a specific game, one must also master the rules of conduct surrounding it. Specifically, one must learn to both win and lose with dignity. In **Liam Wins the Game, Sometimes**, Liam challenges his father to a board game. Understandably, as long as Liam wins the game, and is receiving the accolades, he is able to show good sportsmanship. However, upon losing, Liam becomes unravelled. This story captures the hilarity of a sore loser, while offering some acceptable responses to defeat. In the end, Liam does **not** win the game—however, he takes pride in his decorum.

This is Liam.

Liam loves playing games. He has "Walk-the-plank," "Cherry Tree," "Rainbow Fish," and "Diving Dragons." His favorite game, though, is "Woof-Woof" which he loves to play with Daddy.

In "Woof-Woof," whoever collects all the bones first, wins. Sometimes Liam finds all the bones before Daddy. Then Liam gets to shout "Woof-Woof, I win!" Liam loves to win. He says, "Good job, Dad."

Daddy loves playing the game too and has fun even though he doesn't always win. When Daddy loses, he says, "Good game, Liam." Daddy is a good sport and fun to play with.

Sometimes, though, Daddy wins. He collects all the bones before Liam. Then Daddy gets to shout, "Woof-Woof, I win!"

Liam does not like it when he doesn't win.
It does not feel good and Liam
does not know what to do.

It is okay to feel disappointed when you don't win. Everyone feels a little frustrated or sad when they don't come in first.

When you lose a game, it is not okay
to moan or cry or throw things.

That kind of behavior is rude. It is being
a poor loser and it spoils the whole game. Others
do not like playing with poor losers.

When you lose, you might say, "Oh rats!" or "Bummer" or "I almost won."

Sometimes you win, and sometimes you don't.
Winning does not make you good,
and losing does not make you bad.

You can congratulate the other player and say "good game." That will make him feel proud. It will make you feel proud too!

Liam is a good sport. Sometimes he wins the game, and sometimes he doesn't. He always knows what to do, though, and that makes him a real **champ**.

Bravo, Liam!